PINGU

Stays in Bed

BBC CHiLDReN'S BOOKS

It was time to get up in Pingu's house. Pingu climbed sleepily out of bed and had a good stretch.

"I could do with a bit more sleep," he yawned.

Pingu was just about to get back in bed when he remembered something.

"Oh, no," he said, gloomily. "It's school today. I don't feel like going to school at all."

"It's too bad," said Pingu, suddenly. "I won't go to school." And he got back into bed and was soon drifting happily off to sleep again.

Meanwhile, Mum, Dad and Pinga were having breakfast.

"Where is Pingu?" said Mum, crossly. "His breakfast is getting cold."

Mum called out loudly, but there was no answer.

It was time for Dad to leave for work. He was going to take Pinga to playschool on his way.

"Come along, little Pinga," said Dad. "We mustn't be late."

Mum looked at the clock and started to tap the table impatiently.

"What is that naughty penguin up to?" she said to herself.

Mum went into Pingu's bedroom only to find Pingu *still* in bed.

"What do you think you're doing, lying in bed? Get up this minute!" said Mum, fiercely. "You're going to be late for school."

"I don't feel well," said Pingu, weakly. "My head hurts."

"Oh, my poor little Pingu," said Mum, gently. "I'll go and get you a nice hot drink."

When Mum had left the room, Pingu sat up in bed
and roared with laughter.

"What a joke!" he said to himself. "It's so easy to
skip school."

Mum made Pingu a hot drink and got the thermometer ready to take his temperature.

"Open wide," said Mum. She popped the
thermometer into Pingu's mouth. "Keep that in for
two minutes."

As soon as Mum had gone, Pingu took the thermometer out of his mouth and peered at it. His temperature didn't look very high. Then he had a brilliant idea. He dipped the thermometer into his hot drink.

"That should do it," he chuckled to himself.

After a while, Mum came back and looked at the thermometer. When she saw the high temperature she looked very alarmed.

"Oh, my goodness," she gasped. "I must send for the doctor immediately."

Mum phoned the doctor.

"Hello," she said, anxiously. "My little penguin has a very high temperature. Can you come at once?"

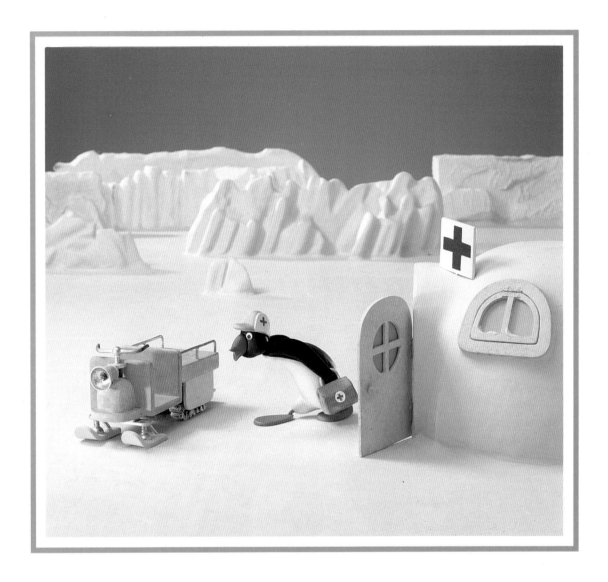

The doctor grabbed his special bag and rushed out of his surgery. He didn't like the sound of Pingu's temperature at all.

In no time he had reached Pingu's house.
"Right, where's the patient?" he asked briskly, as
he came charging through the door.

The doctor examined Pingu carefully with a stethoscope and then peered into his mouth.

"Just keep still," said the doctor, kindly. "There's nothing to worry about."

The doctor was puzzled. He couldn't actually find anything wrong with Pingu. He scratched his head and wondered what the trouble could be.

Pingu sat on the bed and tried to look as ill as possible.

19

At last the doctor turned to Mum. "Could I have a word with you outside?" he whispered.

Mum looked very worried. "Is it serious?"

"Well, it's rather strange," said the doctor.

Mum and the doctor left the room. Pingu lay in
bed getting more and more worried. He hated
waiting. After a while, he decided to go and listen
at the door. He couldn't hear anything.

Then he peered through the keyhole. What he saw made him jump back in alarm. The doctor was explaining something to Mum and was holding an enormous syringe in his hand.

"Oh, help!" shrieked Pingu, waving his arms about in horror. "I hate injections. What can I do?"

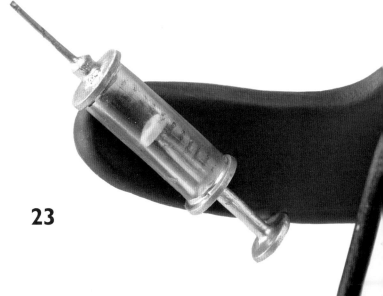

23

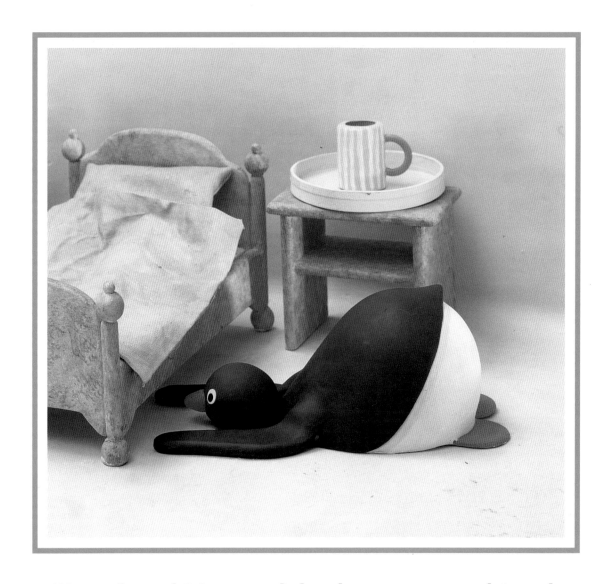

Pingu heard Mum and the doctor approaching the door. There was nothing else for it. In a flash, Pingu dived under the bed.

"That's odd," said Mum when she saw the empty bed. "He can't have gone very far, particularly as he's not feeling well. Perhaps he's in the bathroom."

While the doctor and Mum went off to look for him, Pingu slid out from under the bed and tried to escape through the door without being seen.

But Mum spotted him.

"Pingu!" she cried. "Come back at once. The doctor thinks you should have a little injection to make you feel better."

Pingu was already at the door with his school satchel on.

"I don't need an injection, thank you. I suddenly feel better," he shouted over his shoulder and dashed off.

Over at Pingu's school, the school teacher was
ringing the bell for the start of class. There was no
sign of Pingu.

Not far away, Pingu was sliding
along on his satchel at top speed.
He felt so relieved to have escaped
the doctor that the idea of school
now seemed rather fun.

He reached his school in record time and leaped into his seat. His classmates turned round and watched him in amazement.

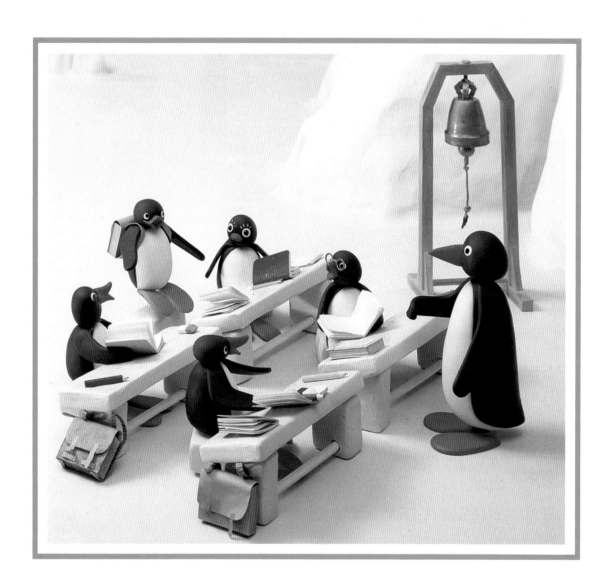

"Good morning, Pingu," said the school teacher, icily.

"Hello, everyone," said Pingu, cheekily. "It's a very good morning. In fact, I've *never* been so glad to come to school before!"

More delightful Pingu stories to read and favourite characters to collect

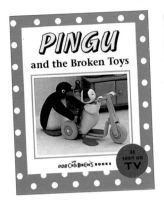

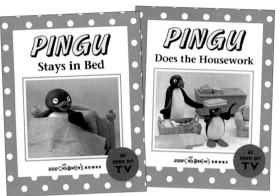

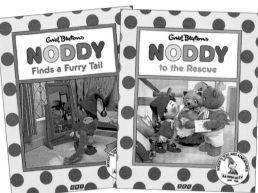

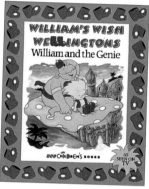

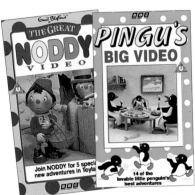

BBC CHILDREN'S PUBLISHING